PASBWARK

W9-AYC-847

PASBWARK

WALT DISNEY

Pinocchio

TWIN BOOKS/HAMLYN

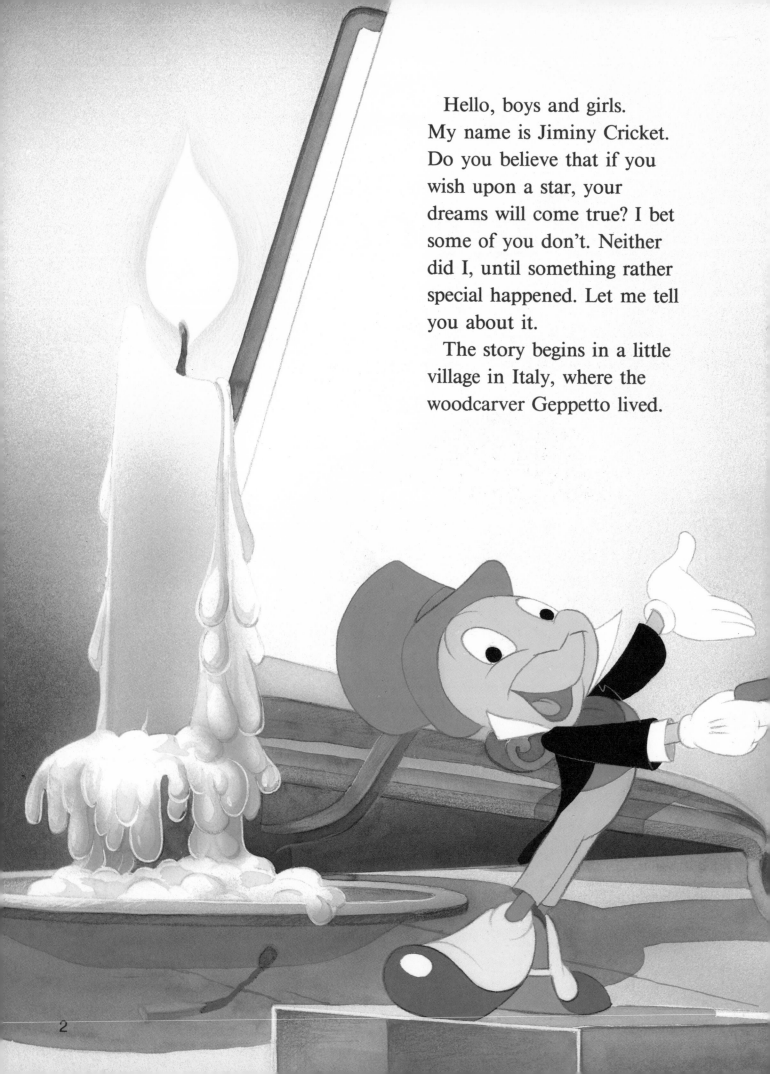

Hello, boys and girls. My name is Jiminy Cricket. Do you believe that if you wish upon a star, your dreams will come true? I bet some of you don't. Neither did I, until something rather special happened. Let me tell you about it.

The story begins in a little village in Italy, where the woodcarver Geppetto lived.

Geppetto made all sorts of
toys out of wood. His shop
was full of cuckoo clocks,
toy ducks, music boxes and
his specialty, puppets.

One of these puppets sat on a table, waiting for the finishing touches. It was a little boy puppet who was missing his eyebrows and mouth.

That afternoon, Gepetto took his brush in hand and started to paint in the eyebrows and mouth.

Geppetto lived with his cat Figaro and his goldfish Cleo. He had always wanted to have a little boy and while he worked on the puppet, he tried to think of a name.

"I've got it. I'll call this one Pinocchio," he said to Figaro.

6

Later on, Geppetto put
Pinocchio away for the night
and got ready for bed. Before
he settled down to sleep,
Geppetto looked out of the
window, at the star-filled sky.
Suddenly he shouted, "Look,
Figaro! Do you see that
really bright star? That's the
Wishing Star."

Figaro stared at the sky. Where Geppetto was pointing, there was a star that was brighter than all the others.

"I'm going to make a wish. I wish that Pinocchio would become a real live boy," said the woodcarver.

While the whole world was tucked away in bed, a bright ray of light shone upon the village. Soon a falling star appeared and followed the ray of light, until it reached Geppetto's house.

A pale blue light filled the workshop and was transformed into the Blue Fairy. She had heard Geppetto's wish.

The Blue Fairy glided across the room: "Pinocchio," she said, "I am the Blue Fairy and I have the power to make wishes come true, Geppetto has wished that you become a real live boy so I shall turn you into a boy – but you will still be made of wood. If you can prove that you are brave, unselfish and able to tell right from wrong, you will become a real live boy."

With a wave of her golden wand, she transformed the puppet into a wooden boy.

Pinocchio opened his eyes and began to move his arms and legs. Opening his mouth, he began to speak. "I can talk! I can walk!" he exclaimed with joy.

Jiminy Cricket, who had been watching was amazed. "Well, I'll be darned! Pinocchio is a real boy!"

The Blue Fairy turned to Jiminy Cricket and said, "there's only one thing missing in Pinocchio – a conscience. Will you accept that role, Jiminy Cricket? Will you help him choose between right and wrong?"

The astounded Jiminy Cricket looked at the Blue Fairy open-mouthed.

"Do you promise to look after Pinocchio, to give him advice and see that he isn't led astray?" the Blue Fairy continued.

"Yes Ma'am" stammered the cricket. "I promise to stay by his side and guide him. But I'm just a poor little cricket and well..."

The Blue Fairy smiled at the cricket and with a wave of her wand changed his ragged clothes into brand-new ones.

Fluttering her wings, the Blue Fairy disappeared, leaving behind a faint ray of blue light.

In the meantime, Geppetto, hearing voices, had come into the workshop. He could hardly believe his eyes – there was his puppet dancing about and singing.

"Am I dreaming? Can this be true? My little Pinocchio is a real boy!" Geppetto cried as he lifted Pinocchio in his arms. "Oh, thank you, Wishing Star, for making my wish come true," said the kind woodcarver, hugging the boy close to him.

Figaro and Cleo came to join in the celebration. Cleo was so excited that she leaped out of her bowl.

"I hope you three are going to be good friends," said Geppetto contentedly.

After a while, exhausted by all the excitement, everyone went back to bed.

The next morning, after breakfast, Geppetto handed Pinocchio some books. "What are these for, Papa?" asked Pinocchio.

Geppetto led Pinocchio to the front door. "See those other children? They are going to school. And since you are a little boy and not a puppet, you, too, must go to school," Geppetto explained.

An apple in one hand, his schoolbooks in the other, Pinocchio strolled off in search of the school.

"If I just follow this road, I'll find the school," he said, happily swinging his books and whistling.

Pinocchio walked through the village, quite unaware that he was being watched by two very suspicious-looking characters.

"Hey! Do you see what I see?" the fox asked. "That's a wooden boy – a puppet that walks and talks – without strings! We can sell him to Stromboli, the stage-manager who is famous for his puppet show", the fox said, rubbing his paws together.

As Pinocchio came closer
the fox tripped him with his
cane.

"Oh! Sorry about that"
said the fox. "Allow me to
introduce myself, I'm
J Worthington Foulfellow –
Honest John to my friends,"
said the fox with a bow "and
this is my friend Gideon," he
added, pointing to the cat.

"Where are you going in such a hurry?" asked J Worthington Foulfellow.

"I'm going to school" said Pinocchio.

"School! What do you want to waste your time going to school for?" asked Gideon with a sneer.

"Yes!" added J Worthington Foulfellow. "A talented young boy like you should be on the stage."

"On the stage? You mean an actor?" said Pinocchio, his eyes round in wonder.

"Yes, the stage. Just think of it – bright lights, the roar of applause – fame! More fun than school!" replied J. Worthington Foulfellow.

"Come with us," said Gideon. "We'll make you a star!"

Meanwhile, Jiminy Cricket, who had been following Pinocchio from a distance, began to worry. He did not like the looks of Pinocchio's two companions and decided not to let Pinocchio out of his sight.

When Jiminy heard the conversation about acting, he was very alarmed. He had promised the Blue Fairy he would look after Pinocchio and wasn't at all sure that playing hooky to go on the stage was what the Blue Fairy had in mind for the little wooden boy.

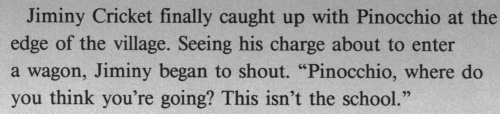

Jiminy Cricket finally caught up with Pinocchio at the edge of the village. Seeing his charge about to enter a wagon, Jiminy began to shout. "Pinocchio, where do you think you're going? This isn't the school."

"Hello, Jiminy Cricket. I'm not going to school today. I'm going to be an actor – a star!" replied Pinocchio. "I'm going to meet Mr Stromboli. He's going to give me a job in his puppet theater."

"Star! What's all this nonsense about the stage? You come down from there this minute! Think of your Papa, Geppetto!" the angry cricket shouted.

Pinocchio paid no attention to Jiminy Cricket and walked into Stromboli's wagon.

Stromboli was delighted with this puppet without strings. Gleefully rubbing his hands together, Stromboli thought of all the money he was going to make.

That evening, Pinocchio made his debut on stage. The crowd was amazed to see a marionette without strings able to dance and sing.

As the applause continued at the end of Pinocchio's performance, Stromboli appeared on the stage and presented him as the marionette with invisible strings. Pinocchio took his bows amid a shower of gold coins.

All this attention went straight to Pinocchio's head — he was stage-struck!

When Pinocchio did not return that afternoon, Geppetto was very worried. When night fell, and there was still no sign of Pinocchio, Geppetto and Figaro went out to search for the wooden boy.

Lantern in hand, Geppetto scoured the village, calling out, "PINOCCHIO! PINOCCHIO!" until his throat was sore. The woodcarver and his cat spent the whole night in the streets, searching high and low, but to no avail.

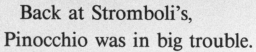

Back at Stromboli's, Pinocchio was in big trouble.

After threatening to use him as firewood, Stromboli had locked Pinocchio in a cage.

Later that night, Jiminy Cricket slipped into the room and climbed up to the cage.

"So this is how you become a star" he whispered, shaking his head sadly.

As Jiminy Cricket struggled with the lock, a dazzling blue light filled the room.

"It's the Blue Fairy!" cried Jiminy Cricket.

"You seem to have gotten off to a bad start, young man," said the Blue Fairy.

"Oh it wasn't my fault," replied Pinocchio. "A giant monster with bulging eyes kidnapped me."

Jiminy Cricket couldn't believe his ears – Pinocchio was telling a lie. Ashamed of his little friend, he covered his ears.

"And what about school?" asked the Blue Fairy.

"School? Ah, well, that was lots of fun" Pinocchio fibbed.

With each lie, Pinocchio's nose grew and grew, until it stretched right through the bars of the cage. Pinocchio cried out in terror.

"Now you see, Pinocchio, a lie grows and grows until it's as plain as the nose on your face" the Blue Fairy explained.

"Oh, I'm terribly sorry. I promise never to tell a lie again," pleaded Pinocchio, trembling with fear.

Seeing that Pinocchio was genuinely sorry, the Blue Fairy waved her wand and unlocked the cage.

"Now remember this lesson. If you want to become a real live boy you have to prove yourself worthy. And you, Jiminy Cricket, you've promised to be his conscience, and I'm counting on you to show him right from wrong," said the Blue Fairy disappearing in a twinkle.

"Come on, we're free!" shouted Jiminy Cricket, leaping from the cage.

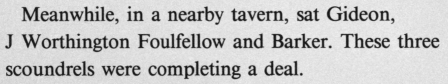

Meanwhile, in a nearby tavern, sat Gideon, J Worthington Foulfellow and Barker. These three scoundrels were completing a deal.

Barker was an evil man who enticed naughty boys away to Pleasure Island to make silly donkeys of themselves and never be allowed to return home.

Foulfellow and Gideon had agreed to help Barker find some boys.

Filling their pockets with gold coins, Foulfellow and Gideon went off in search of victims.

No sooner had they stepped outside the tavern than who should walk by but Pinocchio. Grabbing Pinocchio with his cane, Foulfellow tipped his hat and said, "Hello there, young man. Where are you off to?"

"I'm going home to Papa," stammered the startled boy.

54

"You look a bit pale. Let me check your pulse," said Foulfellow, taking Pinocchio's wrist.

"Ah! Just as I thought. You can't possibly go home in this state. What you need is rest and relaxation. And I know just the spot for that," exclaimed the crafty fox.

"Yes, he should go to Pleasure Island," added Gideon.

"Pleasure Island?" asked Pinocchio.

"You'll love it. It's a wonderful place," insisted Foulfellow.

Leading Pinocchio along,
the two rascals filled his head
with promises of games and
toys and all the candies he
could eat.

Jiminy Cricket followed
from a distance, wondering
what Pinocchio was up to
now.

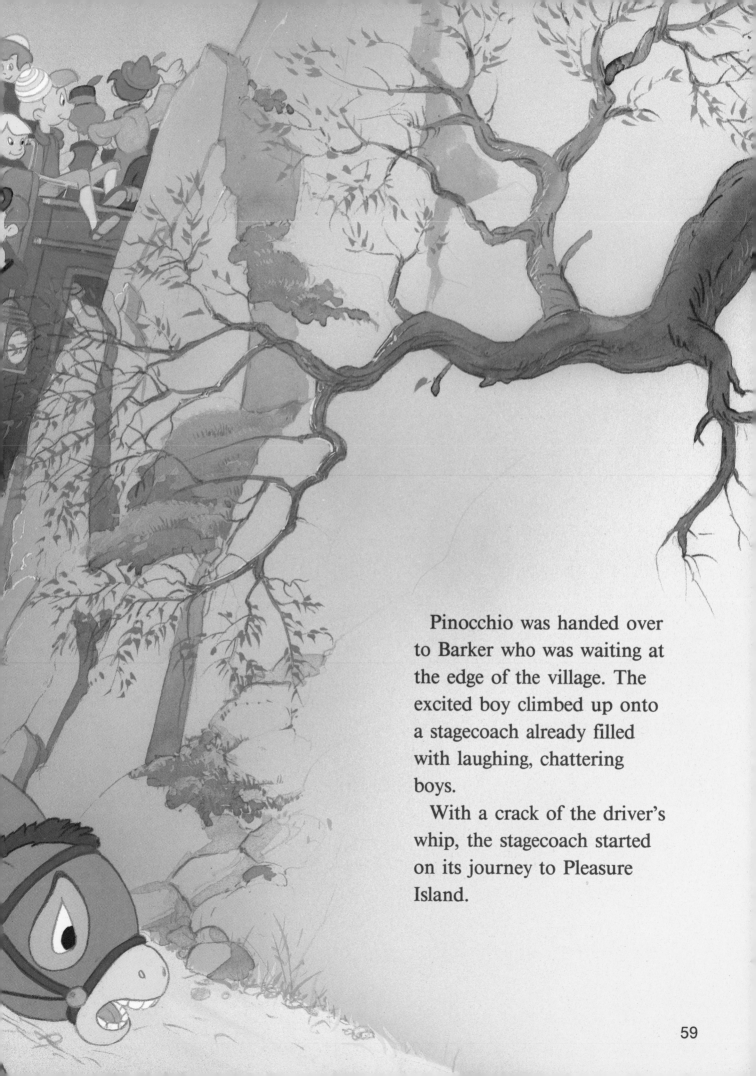

Pinocchio was handed over to Barker who was waiting at the edge of the village. The excited boy climbed up onto a stagecoach already filled with laughing, chattering boys.

With a crack of the driver's whip, the stagecoach started on its journey to Pleasure Island.

By nightfall the coach reached the port where a ferry was waiting to take it across to the island. During the crossing, Pinocchio made friends with a boy called Lampwick.

As the boat neared the island, the boys started to cheer at the sight of an enormous amusement park.

"Look at all those cigarettes and cigars!" shouted Pinocchio.

"Yeah," said Lampwick, "I hear that nothing is forbidden here. No grownups to say, "no," he added, as they ran down the gangplank and on to the mysterious island.

"If my mother could see me now, she'd have a fit,"
said Lampwick, helping himself to a huge sandwich.
"Now I can eat whatever and whenever I like.
Want a bite?" he asked Pinocchio.

His friend shook his head. He was too busy trying to
eat both a lollipop, and a candy cane at the same time.

While Pinocchio stuffed himsef with candy, Jiminy Cricket was exploring the island. Hearing shouts, he crept up behind Barker, who was giving orders to his henchmen.

"As soon as those brats turn into donkeys, I want you to round them up. They should be down in the salt mines by daybreak!" yelled Barker cracking his whip.

"Donkeys! Salt mines!" "I'd better get Pinocchio out of here — and fast," said Jiminy Cricket, running off to warn his friend.

Jiminy found Pinocchio in the pool hall, playing with Lampwick.

When Jiminy Cricket told Pinocchio what he'd heard, the two boys just began to laugh.

"Hey! Who's this pest?"
asked Lampwick. "Why
don't ya get lost?"

"All right!" said the
indignant Jiminy Cricket.
"Turn into donkeys. See if I
care," he added, as he
stomped off.

The two boys continued to giggle and to mock Jiminy Cricket. "You'd think something bad was going to happen," laughed Lampwick.

No sooner had he said this than he sprouted donkey's ears.

While Pinocchio looked on open-mouthed, Lampwick grew a tail and his feet turned into hooves.

Not noticing what was happening to him, Lampwick still went on laughing.

Suddenly, Lampwick's laugh turned into a hee-haw.
Looking into the mirror, he saw that he had been
completely transformed into a donkey. He jumped down
from the pool table with a clatter and galloped around
in a great panic.

Pinocchio, too, had sprouted donkey's ears and a tail
and was very frightened.

Hearing Pinocchio's frantic cries, Jiminy Cricket
rushed to his aid. "Quick! Let's get out of here!" the
cricket yelled.

Pinocchio and Jiminy Cricket raced across the now-deserted island, leaping over mounds of candy and toys, they ran as fast as they could.

"Faster, Pinocchio! We have to get off this island before daybreak," urged the cricket.

Finally they reached the cliff overlooking the sea.
Pinocchio dove in and Jiminy followed, using his
umbrella as a parachute.

Being made of wood, Pinocchio immediately rose to
the surface and began to float. The cricket jumped on
to his back and the current carried them towards the
mainland.

The bedraggled pair finally reached the shore at
sunrise. Shaking the water out of his hat, Jiminy Cricket
noticed a floating bottle. "Pinocchio! Grab that bottle.
There's a message in it," shouted the cricket.

Doing as he was told, Pinocchio reached for the bottle
and pulled out a piece of paper.

Jiminy Cricket began to read the message. "It's from
Geppetto. He says he was on his way to Pleasure Island
when Monstro the Whale swallowed his boat."

"I'm going to save my
Papa from that nasty whale,"
Pinocchio said, running
towards the water.

"Wait a minute!" yelled
Jiminy Cricket. "You can't
search underwater–you're
made of wood and you'll
float."

"Not with this stone
weighing me down," replied
Pinocchio, as he jumped into
the water.

Once at the bottom of the
ocean, Jiminy and Pinocchio
began their search for
Monstro.

Suddenly an enormous
shadow covered the ocean
floor. Looking up through
the water, Pinocchio and
Jiminy were terrified to see
Monstro looming
threateningly overhead.

Pinocchio untied the stone and floated up towards the whale. Just at that moment, Monstro was about to eat lunch and, opening his gigantic jaws, sucked in a whole school of fish as well as the struggling Pinocchio.

Meanwhile, Jiminy Cricket banged on the whale's closed teeth, yelling, "come on Blubbermouth. Open up."

Pinocchio swam with the fish down the whale's throat into his cavern-like belly. There he saw Geppetto and Figaro fishing from the side of the boat.

When Geppetto pulled in his fishing net, he had quite a surprise. There, among the squirming, wriggling fish, was his dear Pinocchio.

Hugging his son in his arms, he cried with joy.

"Papa," said Pinocchio "I've come to rescue you."

"Oh, my dear son. If only it was possible to escape from here," Geppetto sighed.

Geppetto noticed
Pinocchio's ears and tail.

"No time to explain now,"
said Pinocchio. "We've got
to get out of here."

"Yes, but how?" asked
Geppetto.

Pinocchio began breaking
up pieces of furniture they
found floating around.
"We'll start a fire. Monstro
will wake up and sneeze and
then we'll be thrown out of
here."

When Monstro began to feel the effects of the fire, he tossed and turned, shaking his gigantic body.

Inside, the captives quickly jumped onto a raft and began to paddle up towards the whale's throat. When they reached the whale's mouth, the way out was barred by his gigantic teeth.

But suddenly Monstro let out an enormous sneeze that blew the raft out into the open seas. There, they were joined by Jiminy Cricket who had just about given them up for lost.

Although free from captivity, they were not out of danger. Monstro was furious and, seeing the raft bobbing up ahead, nose-dived under the water. For an instant it seemed as if he had disappeared, but the whale's giant flipper whipped up under the raft, tossing it in the air and smashing it to pieces.

Pinocchio grabbed Geppetto, who was barely
conscious, and carried him on his back. "Leave me.
Save yourself," the old man moaned.

Eventually, they were washed up on shore. Regaining
consciousness, Geppetto looked around to see if
everyone was there and saw Pinocchio lying face down
in the water.

"My boy," Geppetto cried, lifting the lifeless body into his arms. The sad group stumbled back to the village.

Geppetto lay Pinocchio on his bed and knelt down at his side. "Little Pinocchio, you risked your life to save me," the old man sobbed.

Suddenly a brilliant blue light lit up the room. The Blue Fairy had arrived.

Waving her magic wand at him, she said, "Wake up Pinocchio. You have proved you are a brave little boy. I shall reward you by giving you life."

The lifeless wooden boy was suddenly transformed into a real live little boy.

Sitting up, Pinocchio blinked his eyes and asked "What's wrong Papa?

"Pinocchio! Pinocchio! You're alive", gasped Geppetto with joy. "You're a real live boy!"

Cleo jumped with joy, while Figaro danced a jig. At last the old man's wish had come true.

Jiminy Cricket watched the happy scene with tears in his eyes. "Well, I guess I'll be moving on now," he said to himself. "And now, I know that wishes do sometimes come true."

Published by Twin Books
17 Sherwood Place
Greenwich, CT 06830
U.S.A.

Copyright © 1986 Disney Productions
Copyright © 1986 Twin Books

Distributed by
Hamlyn Publishing
a division of The Hamlyn Publishing Group Limited
Bridge House, London Road
Twickenham, Middlesex
England

All rights reserved. No part of this publication
may be reproduced, stored in a retrieval system
or transmitted in any form by any means,
electronic, mechanical, photocopying or otherwise,
without first obtaining written permission of the
copyright owner.

ISBN 0 600 31182 1

Printed in Hong Kong